THE DETECTIVE

MD. ADEEL ASHRAF

To all the readers who have ever lost themselves in the pages of a book, this one is for you. Your passion for stories and the written word has inspired me to become a writer, and I am eternally grateful for your love and support.

To my family and friends, thank you for standing by me through the highs and lows of this journey. Your unwavering belief in me has kept me going, and I could not have done this without you.

And finally, to the characters who have taken on a life of their own in these pages, thank you for sharing your stories with me. You have made me laugh, cry, and feel every emotion in between. It has been an honor to bring your voices to the world, and I hope that others will love and cherish you as much as I do.

With love and gratitude,

Md.Adeel Ashraf

Contents

Foreword

It is with great pleasure that I introduce this first installment of the "Detectives" book series, a compilation of ten murder mystery dramas that will keep you on the edge of your seat from start to finish. As a lover of crime fiction, I have always been fascinated by the intricate details of murder investigations and the brilliant minds of the detectives who solve them.

In "Detectives", you'll meet a diverse cast of characters, from hard-nosed detectives to brilliant young investigators, each with their own unique style and approach to solving crime. Set in locations ranging from bustling cities to sleepy villages, each story is meticulously crafted to draw you in and keep you guessing until the very end.

The beauty of murder mysteries lies in their ability to take readers on a journey of discovery, piecing together clues and following the twists and turns of the investigation until the truth is finally revealed. And in this compilation, you'll find ten such journeys, each one expertly crafted to keep you engaged and entertained from the first page to the last.

As you read these stories, I invite you to immerse yourself in the world of crime fiction, to embrace the thrill of the chase and the satisfaction of a well-solved case. And who knows, you may even pick up a thing or two about detective work along the way.

So sit back, relax, and let the "Detectives" take you on a journey of intrigue, suspense, and murder. I promise, you won't be disappointed

Acknowledgements

Writing a book is a journey that cannot be taken alone. It takes a village of people to make a book possible, and I am grateful to the many individuals who have supported me throughout this process.

First and foremost, I would like to thank my family and friends for their unwavering love and encouragement. Your belief in me has kept me going through the highs and lows of this journey, and I could not have done this without you.

I would also like to thank the many individuals who have supported me in various ways, from offering words of encouragement to helping with research or providing feedback on early drafts. Your contributions have been invaluable, and I am grateful for your generosity.

And finally, I would like to express my gratitude to the readers who have taken the time to read this book. Your support means the world to me, and I am humbled and honored to share my story with you.

With gratitude,
Md.Adeel Ashraf

CHAPTER ONE

The Death of Mr. Johnson

Characters:

Detective Anderson
Mr. Johnson's wife, Mrs. Johnson
Mr. Johnson's business partner, Mr. Smith
Mr. Johnson's assistant, Ms. Jones

Act I

Detective Anderson enters the crime scene, where Mr. Johnson's body lies on the floor.

Detective Anderson: What happened here? Who discovered the body?

Mrs. Johnson: (crying) I did. I came home and found my husband lying on the floor.

Detective Anderson: Can you tell me if

anything unusual happened before you found him?

Mrs. Johnson: No, everything was normal. He was supposed to be at a business meeting, but he canceled it.

Mr. Smith: I was supposed to meet with Mr. Johnson today, but he canceled at the last minute. I thought it was strange.

Ms. Jones: (nervously) I was with Mr. Johnson this morning, but I left around 10 a.m. to run errands.

Detective Anderson: (to Ms. Jones) Can you tell me more about your relationship with Mr. Johnson?

Ms. Jones: We had a professional relationship. I was his assistant and helped him with his work.

Act II

Detective Anderson investigates the crime scene and finds evidence of a struggle.

Detective Anderson: Mrs. Johnson, did your husband have any enemies?

Mrs. Johnson: No, everyone loved him. He was a kind and generous man.

Mr. Smith: (defensively) We had some disagreements about the business, but it was nothing serious.

Ms. Jones: (quietly) I don't know of anyone who would want to harm him.

Detective Anderson: (skeptically) Really? Because it seems like there was a struggle here.

Ms. Jones: (looking guilty) Okay, fine. There was an argument this morning. Mr. Johnson found out that I had been embezzling money from the company.

Mrs. Johnson: (shocked) How could you do something like that?

Ms. Jones: (tearfully) I had some debts to pay off, and I thought I could get away with it.

Mr. Smith: (angrily) You're responsible for Mr. Johnson's death! You should be arrested!

Detective Anderson: (calmly) Let's not jump to conclusions. Ms. Jones, can you tell me where you were when Mr. Johnson was killed?

Ms. Jones: I was at the bank, depositing the money I had stolen. I have the receipt to prove it.

Detective Anderson: (nodding) That checks

out. Mr. Smith, do you have any alibi?

Mr. Smith: (nervously) I was at home, but I don't have anyone to vouch for me.

Act III

Detective Anderson reviews the evidence and interviews the suspects again.

Detective Anderson: Based on the evidence and testimony, I have a good idea of what happened. Mr. Smith, you had a motive to kill Mr. Johnson because of your disagreements about the business.

Mr. Smith: (defensively) That's not true! We were just arguing about a business deal.

Detective Anderson: I also have evidence that places you at the scene of the crime, including your fingerprints on the murder weapon.

Mr. Smith: (resigned) Okay, fine. I did it. I couldn't take it anymore. He was always trying to control everything.

Mrs. Johnson: (sobbing) How could you do this? He was my husband!

Ms. Jones: (quietly) I'm sorry for my part in this. I never meant

CHAPTER TWO

The Mysterious Case of the Poisoned Cup

Characters:

Detective Williams
Victim's wife, Mrs. Parker
Victim's business partner, Mr. Peterson
Victim's housekeeper, Ms. Brown

Act I

Detective Williams arrives at the scene of the crime, where Mr. Parker's body is lying on the floor.

Detective Williams: What happened here? Who discovered the body?

Mrs. Parker: (crying) I did. I came home from running errands and found my husband lying on the floor.

Detective Williams: Can you tell me if anything unusual happened before you found him?

Mrs. Parker: No, everything was normal. He was supposed to be at a business meeting, but it got canceled.

Mr. Peterson: I was supposed to meet with Mr. Parker today, but he canceled at the last minute. I thought it was strange.

Ms. Brown: (nervously) I found a cup on the floor near the body. It looked like it had some kind of liquid in it.

Detective Williams: (to Ms. Brown) Can you show me where you found the cup?

Ms. Brown leads Detective Williams to the cup on the floor.

Detective Williams: (examining the cup) This looks like it might be the murder weapon. I'm going to take it for analysis.

Act II

Detective Williams investigates the crime scene and sends the cup to the lab for analysis.

Detective Williams: Mrs. Parker, did your husband have any enemies?

Mrs. Parker: No, he was a kind man who got along with everyone.

Mr. Peterson: (defensively) We had some disagreements about the business, but it was nothing serious.

Ms. Brown: (quietly) I don't know of anyone who would want to harm him.

Detective Williams: (skeptically) Really? Because it seems like someone wanted to harm him.

Ms. Brown: (looking guilty) Okay, fine. I might have seen something. I saw Mr. Peterson arguing with Mr. Parker about the business this morning.

Mr. Peterson: (angrily) That's not true! We were just discussing the new deal we were working on.

Mrs. Parker: (confused) What deal? My husband never mentioned anything about a new deal.

Act III

Detective Williams reviews the evidence and interviews the suspects again.

Detective Williams: Based on the evidence and

testimony, I have a good idea of what happened. Ms. Brown, can you tell me what you saw?

Ms. Brown: I saw Mr. Peterson arguing with Mr. Parker this morning. Then, later on, I saw Mr. Peterson come back to the house with a cup that looked like the one near the body.

Detective Williams: Mr. Peterson, do you have anything to say to that?

Mr. Peterson: (hesitantly) Okay, fine. I did go back to the house, but I didn't kill him. I just wanted to talk to him about the deal.

Detective Williams: (nodding) That's what I thought. But the lab results came back, and the cup had traces of a lethal poison in it. Do you have anything to say to that?

Mr. Peterson: (looking shocked) I didn't poison the cup! I only brought it back to talk to him!

Mrs. Parker: (crying) How could you do this to my husband?

Detective Williams: (calmly) I think we're done here. Mr. Peterson, you're under arrest for the murder of Mr. Parker. Anything you say can and will be used against you in a court of law.

CHAPTER THREE

The Case of the Missing Heir

Characters:

Detective Smith
Victim's wife, Mrs. Anderson
Victim's business partner, Mr. Collins
Victim's sister, Ms. Jackson

Act I

Detective Smith arrives at the scene of the crime, where Mr. Anderson's body is lying on the floor.

Detective Smith: What happened here? Who discovered the body?

Mrs. Anderson: (crying) I did. I came home from running errands and found my husband lying on the floor.

Detective Smith: Can you tell me if anything unusual happened before you found him?

Mrs. Anderson: No, everything was normal. He was supposed to be at a business meeting, but it got canceled.

Mr. Collins: I was supposed to meet with Mr. Anderson today, but he canceled at the last minute. I thought it was strange.

Ms. Jackson: (nervously) My brother was supposed to leave me a substantial inheritance in his will. I hope this isn't foul play.

Detective Smith: (to Ms. Jackson) Can you tell me more about the inheritance?

Ms. Jackson: My brother was a wealthy man, and he promised to leave me a large sum of money in his will.

Act II

Detective Smith investigates the crime scene and finds no clear evidence of foul play.

Detective Smith: Mrs. Anderson, did your husband have any enemies?

Mrs. Anderson: No, he was a kind man who got along with everyone.

Mr. Collins: (defensively) We had some disagreements about the business, but it was nothing serious.

Ms. Jackson: (anxiously) I don't know of anyone who would want to harm him.

Detective Smith: (skeptically) Really? Because it seems like someone wanted to harm him.

Act III

Detective Smith reviews the evidence and interviews the suspects again.

Detective Smith: Based on the evidence and testimony, I have a good idea of what happened. Ms. Jackson, can you tell me more about the inheritance?

Ms. Jackson: (hesitantly) Well, my brother was a bit of a gambler. He had some debts, and I helped him pay them off in exchange for the promise of the inheritance.

Detective Smith: (nodding) That's what I thought. But here's the thing: there's no sign of forced entry or a struggle, and the only thing missing from the house is the will. I think someone stole it.

Mrs. Anderson: (shocked) Who would do such

a thing?

Mr. Collins: (defensively) It wasn't me. I had no reason to steal the will.

Ms. Jackson: (looking guilty) I... I might know something.

Detective Smith: (leaning in) What is it?

Ms. Jackson: (quietly) I overheard my brother and Mr. Collins talking about the inheritance. They were arguing about the terms of the will, and then I heard a loud thud. When I went to check, Mr. Collins was leaving the house in a hurry.

Detective Smith: (nodding) That's all I need to hear. Mr. Collins, you're under arrest for the theft of the will and the murder of Mr. Anderson. Anything you say can and will be used against you in a court of law.

Mr. Collins: (defiantly) You have no evidence! You can't prove anything!

Detective Smith: (smiling) Actually, we do. We found your fingerprints on the safe where the will was kept, and Ms. Jackson's testimony puts you at the scene of the crime. You're going away for a long

CHAPTER FOUR

The Case of the Poisoned Pudding

Characters:

Detective Johnson
Victim's husband, Mr. White
Victim's sister, Ms. Black
Victim's best friend, Ms. Green

Act I

Detective Johnson arrives at the scene of the crime, where Ms. White's body is lying on the floor.

Detective Johnson: What happened here? Who discovered the body?

Mr. White: I did. I came home from work and found my wife lying on the floor.

Detective Johnson: Can you tell me if anything unusual happened before you found her?

Mr. White: No, everything was normal. We had dinner together, and she said she wasn't feeling well. I went to work, and when I came back, I found her like this.

Ms. Black: (sobbing) My sister was the kindest person I know. Who could do such a thing?

Ms. Green: (concerned) This is so unlike her. She was always so careful about what she ate.

Detective Johnson: (to Mr. White) Can you tell me what you had for dinner?

Mr. White: (nervously) We had pudding for dessert. My wife made it herself.

Act II

Detective Johnson investigates the crime scene and finds a vial of poison hidden in the kitchen.

Detective Johnson: (to Ms. Black) Did your sister have any enemies?

Ms. Black: No, she was loved by everyone who knew her.

Ms. Green: (hesitantly) Well, there was one person who didn't like her very much.

Detective Johnson: Who?

Ms. Green: (reluctantly) Her ex-boyfriend, Mr. Brown. He was jealous of her marriage to Mr. White.

Detective Johnson: (nodding) I'll have to talk to him. But first, let's talk about that pudding. Do you know what was in it?

Mr. White: Just some milk, sugar, and vanilla. My wife loved making it.

Detective Johnson: (skeptically) That's it? Because I found a vial of poison in your kitchen.

Act III

Detective Johnson reviews the evidence and interviews the suspects again.

Detective Johnson: (to Mr. White) You said your wife made the pudding, but I don't believe you. The poison was in the pudding, which means someone put it there. Who had access to the kitchen?

Mr. White: (looking guilty) I... I did.

Ms. Black: (shocked) What are you saying?

Ms. Green: (alarmed) You wouldn't hurt your own wife, would you?

Detective Johnson: (sternly) It looks like he did. Mr. White, you're under arrest for the murder of your wife, Ms. White. You have the right to remain silent. Anything you say can and will be used against you in a court of law.

Mr. White: (defiantly) I didn't do it! You have no proof!

Detective Johnson: Actually, we do. The poison was traced back to a bottle that you purchased the day before. And the fact that you lied about making the pudding is a clear indication of your guilt.

Ms. Black: (sobbing) How could you do this to my sister?

Ms. Green: (disgusted) You're a monster.

Detective Johnson: (nodding) Unfortunately, some people are capable of terrible things. It's our job to bring them to justice

CHAPTER FIVE

The Case of the Missing Heirloom

Characters:

Detective Smith
Wealthy widow, Mrs. Smith
Mrs. Smith's housekeeper, Mrs. Johnson
Mrs. Smith's nephew, Mr. Brown

Act I

Detective Smith arrives at Mrs. Smith's mansion to investigate the theft of a valuable heirloom.

Detective Smith: Mrs. Smith, can you tell me what happened?

Mrs. Smith: (upset) My late husband's pocket watch has gone missing. It's worth a fortune, and I can't find it anywhere.

Detective Smith: Do you have any idea who might have taken it?

Mrs. Smith: (hesitantly) Well, my nephew, Mr. Brown, was here earlier. He's been having some financial problems lately.

Mrs. Johnson: (chiming in) And he's always been jealous of Mrs. Smith's wealth.

Detective Smith: I'll have to talk to him. Do you mind if I take a look around?

Mrs. Smith: Of course not. Please, do what you have to do.

Act II

Detective Smith searches the mansion and interviews the suspects.

Detective Smith: (to Mr. Brown) So, you were here earlier today. Did you see the pocket watch?

Mr. Brown: (defensively) No, I didn't. I'm not a thief, Detective.

Mrs. Johnson: (skeptically) That's not what you said when you saw the watch last time.

Mr. Brown: (nervously) What do you mean?

Mrs. Johnson: (accusingly) I heard you say you would do anything to get your hands on it.

Detective Smith: (raising an eyebrow) Is that true, Mr. Brown?

Mr. Brown: (flustered) I... I was joking. I would never steal from my own family.

Act III

Detective Smith investigates further and finds a surprising lead.

Detective Smith: (to Mrs. Johnson) Do you know if anyone else has been in the mansion today?

Mrs. Johnson: (thinking) Well, there was a man who came by earlier, looking for donations for a local charity.

Detective Smith: (interested) Can you describe him?

Mrs. Johnson: (remembering) He was tall, with dark hair and a scar on his cheek. He was wearing a blue suit.

Detective Smith: (nodding) That's our man. I think we've found our thief.

Act IV

Detective Smith tracks down the thief and makes a shocking discovery.

Detective Smith: (to the thief) You're under arrest for stealing Mrs. Smith's pocket watch. Do you have anything to say for yourself?

Thief: (smiling) You'll never find it. I sold it to a collector already.

Detective Smith: (surprised) A collector? Who?

Thief: (slyly) A man named Mr. Smith.

Detective Smith: (stunned) Mr. Smith? Mrs. Smith's late husband?

Thief: (laughing) That's right. He came to me a few weeks ago and asked me to steal the pocket watch. He said it was a test to see if his wife was trustworthy.

Detective Smith: (shocked) You mean to tell me that Mrs. Smith's late husband faked his own death and set up this whole thing just to test her loyalty?

Thief: (smiling) Looks like it. And from the looks of it, she passed with flying colors.

Detective Smith: (shaking his head in disbelief)

Well,

CHAPTER SIX

The Murder at The Manor House

Characters:

Detective Charlotte Smith - a young and brilliant detective with a passion for solving crimes.

Lord Edward Blackwood - the owner of the manor house where the murder occurred.

Lady Elizabeth Blackwood - Lord Blackwood's wife.

Miss Anne Grey - Lady Blackwood's personal maid.

Mr. James Reynolds - Lord Blackwood's business partner.

Act 1

(Scene 1)

The scene opens in the grand hall of the manor house. Detective Charlotte Smith is standing near the entrance while Lord and Lady Blackwood are standing next to her. Miss Grey is standing at a distance.

Detective Smith: (Addressing the group) "Can you tell me what happened last night?"

Lord Blackwood: "My wife and I were having a dinner party. Our business partner, Mr. Reynolds, was also present. After dinner, we retired to the sitting room for drinks. It was then that we discovered Miss Grey lying unconscious on the floor."

Lady Blackwood: "She had been hit on the head with a vase, Detective. It was a horrific sight."

(Scene 2)

The scene shifts to the sitting room. Detective Smith is examining the crime scene while Lord and Lady Blackwood and Mr. Reynolds are standing at a distance.

Detective Smith: "Do you know of anyone who would want to harm Miss Grey?"

Lord Blackwood: "No, Detective. She is a valued member of our staff. We cannot think of anyone who would want to hurt her."

Mr. Reynolds: "I agree, Detective. Miss Grey is a hardworking and loyal employee. I cannot imagine who would do such a thing."

(Scene 3)

The scene shifts to Miss Grey's room. Detective Smith is interrogating her.

Detective Smith: "Miss Grey, can you tell me what happened last night?"

Miss Grey: "I don't remember, Detective. The last thing I remember is serving dinner to the guests."

Detective Smith: "Did you notice anything unusual?"

Miss Grey: "No, Detective. Everything was normal. The guests were enjoying their dinner, and there was no argument or anything."

Act 2

(Scene 1)

The scene opens in the library of the manor house. Detective Smith is talking to Lord Blackwood.

Detective Smith: "Lord Blackwood, I have reason to believe that Miss Grey's attack was not a random act. Someone had a motive for harming her."

Lord Blackwood: "What motive could anyone have for harming a maid?"

Detective Smith: "I am not sure yet, but I will find out. In the meantime, I would like to ask you a few questions about Mr. Reynolds."

Lord Blackwood: "What about him?"

Detective Smith: "I believe he had a financial dispute with you recently."

Lord Blackwood: "Yes, that is true. We had a disagreement over some business matters, but it was nothing serious."

Detective Smith: "I see. Do you think it's possible that Mr. Reynolds could have been involved in Miss Grey's attack?"

Lord Blackwood: "I cannot say for sure, Detective. But I find it hard to believe that he would stoop so low as to harm a member of our staff."

(Scene 2)

The scene shifts to Mr. Reynolds' room. Detective Smith is interrogating him.

Detective Smith: "Mr. Reynolds, I understand that you had a financial dispute with Lord Blackwood recently."

Mr. Reynolds: "Yes, that is true, Detective. We had a disagreement over some business matters, but it was nothing serious."

Detective Smith: "I see. And where were you last night when Miss Grey was attacked?"

Mr. Reynolds: "I was in my room, Detective. I retired early because I had an early morning meeting."

Detective Smith: "Can anyone corroborate your alibi?"

Mr. Reynolds: "No, I was alone in my room. But I swear to you, Detective, I had nothing to do with Miss Grey's attack. It's a terrible thing that's happened, and I hope you catch whoever did it."

(Scene 3)

The scene shifts to the grand hall. Detective Smith has gathered everyone together to reveal the killer's identity.

Detective Smith: "Ladies and gentlemen, after a thorough investigation, I have discovered the identity of the person who attacked Miss Grey last night. And that person is none other than Lady Blackwood."

Lady Blackwood: "What? How dare you accuse me of such a thing!"

Detective Smith: "The evidence speaks for itself, Lady Blackwood. I found traces of Miss Grey's blood on your dress, and I discovered a motive for your crime."

Lord Blackwood: "What motive?"

Detective Smith: "I found out that Miss Grey was aware of your affair with Mr. Reynolds, Lady Blackwood. She had threatened to tell Lord Blackwood about it, and that's why you attacked her."

Lady Blackwood: "I...I don't know what to say. I'm sorry, I didn't mean to hurt her."

Lord Blackwood: "You have disgraced our family, Elizabeth. I will make sure you face the consequences of your actions."

Miss Grey: "Thank you, Detective. I'm glad justice has been served."

Epilogue

The scene shifts to Detective Smith's office. She is sitting at her desk, going through some papers when there is a knock on the door.

Detective Smith: "Come in."

A young man enters the room.

Young man: "Excuse me, Detective. My name is William Blackwood. I'm Lord and Lady Blackwood's son."

Detective Smith: "Yes, I know who you are. What can I do for you?"

William Blackwood: "I just wanted to thank you for solving the case. I know it must have been difficult, but you did a great job."

Detective Smith: "Thank you, William. It's my job to solve these cases and bring justice to the victims."

William Blackwood: "I know, but not all detectives are as dedicated as you are. I just wanted you to know that my family and I appreciate your hard work."

Detective Smith: "Thank you, William. That means a lot to me."

The scene ends with Detective Smith smiling at William Blackwood and returning to her work.

The Mysterious Murder at Blackwood Manor

Characters:

1.Detective James Anderson

2.Sir Reginald Blackwood

3.Lady Elizabeth Blackwood

4.Mr. Jonathan Blackwood

5.Ms. Abigail Blackwood

6.Dr. Arthur Davies

7.Miss Sarah Evans

8.Mr. Charles Smith

Act 1:

The stage is set in the grand living room of Blackwood Manor. Sir Reginald Blackwood is hosting a dinner party to celebrate his 60th birthday. The guests arrive, and they are introduced to each other.

Sir Reginald Blackwood: Welcome, everyone, to my humble abode. Please make yourselves at home.

Lady Elizabeth Blackwood: Thank you, dear. The house looks magnificent tonight.

Mr. Jonathan Blackwood: Father, happy birthday. You look as youthful as ever.

Ms. Abigail Blackwood: Yes, happy birthday, grandfather. We hope you have a wonderful day.

Dr. Arthur Davies: Happy birthday, Sir Reginald. It's an honor to be here.

Miss Sarah Evans: Indeed. Happy birthday, Sir Reginald.

Mr. Charles Smith: Happy birthday, sir. May you live to see many more.

As the dinner progresses, the conversation flows smoothly. However, the atmosphere turns tense when Sir Reginald suddenly chokes on his food and falls to the ground.

Lady Elizabeth Blackwood: Reginald! Are you okay?

Mr. Jonathan Blackwood: Father, what happened? Can you hear me?

Ms. Abigail Blackwood: Oh my God! Is he dead?

Dr. Arthur Davies rushes over to check on Sir Reginald.

Dr. Arthur Davies: I'm afraid he's gone. He must have been poisoned.

Detective James Anderson enters the room.

Detective James Anderson: Ladies and gentlemen, I'm Detective James Anderson, and I'm here to investigate the murder of Sir Reginald Blackwood.

Act 2:

Detective Anderson begins his investigation and questions each guest.

Detective James Anderson: Ms. Abigail Blackwood, can you tell me what you were doing when Sir Reginald was poisoned?

Ms. Abigail Blackwood: I was sitting at the table, eating my food.

Detective James Anderson: Mr. Charles Smith, can you tell me what you were doing when Sir Reginald was poisoned?

Mr. Charles Smith: I was sitting at the table, talking to Lady Elizabeth.

Detective James Anderson: Dr. Arthur Davies, can you tell me what you were doing when Sir Reginald was poisoned?

Dr. Arthur Davies: I rushed over to check on him when he fell.

Detective James Anderson: Miss Sarah Evans, can you tell me what you were doing when Sir Reginald was poisoned?

Miss Sarah Evans: I was sitting at the table, sipping my wine.

Detective James Anderson: Lady Elizabeth Blackwood, can you tell me what you were doing when Sir Reginald was poisoned?

Lady Elizabeth Blackwood: I was sitting at the table, talking to Mr. Smith.

Detective James Anderson: Mr. Jonathan Blackwood, can you tell me what you were doing when Sir Reginald was poisoned?

Mr. Jonathan Blackwood: I was pouring myself a glass of wine.

Detective Anderson looks at each guest carefully and observes their behavior.

Detective James Anderson: Ladies and gentlemen, I'm afraid I have bad news. One of you is the murderer.

The guests look at each other in shock.

Act 3:

Detective Anderson reveals the killer's identity.

Detective James Anderson: The murderer is none other than Mr. Jonathan Blackwood.

Ms. Abigail Blackwood: Jonathan, what? Why did you do this?

Mr. Jonathan Blackwood: I'm sorry, but it had to be done. Father was going to disinherit me and leave everything to my siblings. I couldn't let that happen. I had to act fast.

Detective James Anderson: Mr. Blackwood, you're under arrest for the murder of Sir Reginald Blackwood.

As Mr. Jonathan Blackwood is taken away in handcuffs, the guests are left to contemplate the events that have just transpired.

Lady Elizabeth Blackwood: I can't believe this happened in our own home.

Dr. Arthur Davies: It's a sad day when family members turn against each other like this.

Miss Sarah Evans: Indeed, it's a tragic end to a once joyful celebration.

Mr. Charles Smith: Let's hope justice is served, and the Blackwood family can find a way to move forward from this tragedy.

As the curtain falls, the audience is left to ponder the consequences of greed and betrayal in this thrilling murder mystery.

CHAPTER EIGHT

The Poisoned Chalice

Characters:

1.Detective Jack Barnes - A seasoned detective who has solved many cases and is known for his unconventional methods.

2.Sarah Johnson - A wealthy businesswoman who owns a large pharmaceutical company.

3.John Taylor - Sarah's business partner and friend.

4.Dr. Rachel Smith - The head of the pharmaceutical research department in Sarah's company.

5.*James Parker - A lab assistant in the pharmaceutical research department.*

6.*Lisa Green - Sarah's personal assistant.*

Act 1:

Scene 1: The story opens with Detective Jack Barnes investigating the death of Sarah Johnson, who was found dead in her office. The room is in a state of disarray, with papers scattered everywhere, and Sarah lying on the floor. The detective begins his investigation by questioning the people who were in the building at the time of the incident.

Detective Barnes: (Questioning Dr. Rachel Smith) What can you tell me about the events leading up to Sarah's death?

Dr. Rachel Smith: I was in my lab when I heard a commotion coming from Sarah's office. I rushed over there and found her lying on the floor. I called for help immediately.

Detective Barnes: (Questioning James Parker) What were you doing at the time of Sarah's death?

James Parker: I was working in the lab. I didn't hear anything until Dr. Smith came in and told me what happened.

Scene 2: The detective then questions John Taylor and Lisa Green, who were both with Sarah before her death.

Detective Barnes: (Questioning John Taylor) What was your relationship with Sarah?

John Taylor: We were business partners and good friends. We had just finished a meeting before her death.

Detective Barnes: (Questioning Lisa Green) What can you tell me about the meeting?

Lisa Green: We were discussing the launch of a new drug. Sarah seemed fine during the meeting, but after it was over, she complained of feeling unwell.

Act 2:

Scene 1: The detective decides to investigate the pharmaceutical company where Sarah and John are co-owners. He finds out that the company has been developing a new drug that could potentially make millions of dollars.

Detective Barnes: (Questioning Sarah's secretary) Can you tell me anything about the new drug that Sarah's company was developing?

Sarah's Secretary: I know that it was supposed to be a revolutionary new drug that could treat a wide range of diseases.

Scene 2: The detective then interviews the lab assistants who were working on the new drug.

Detective Barnes: (Questioning a lab assistant) Do you know if Sarah was involved in the development of the new drug?

Lab Assistant: I don't know. We were all working on it, but I never saw Sarah in the lab.

Scene 3: The detective discovers that the new drug has not yet been approved by the regulatory agency, and that there were concerns about its safety.

Detective Barnes: (Questioning Dr. Rachel Smith) Were there any safety concerns with the new drug?

Dr. Rachel Smith: There were some concerns, but we were confident that we could resolve them before the drug was released.

Act 3:

Scene 1: The detective then discovers that Sarah's drink was laced with a deadly poison. He suspects that the killer is someone in the pharmaceutical company.

Detective Barnes: (Questioning Lisa Green) Did you see anyone near Sarah's drink before she drank it?

Lisa Green: No, I didn't see anyone near her drink.

Scene 2: The detective then realizes that John Taylor had the most to gain from Sarah's death, as he would inherit her share of the company.

Detective Barnes: (Questioning John Taylor) Did you have any motive for wanting Sarah dead?

John Taylor: No, absolutely not. Sarah was my friend and business partner. I had no reason to harm her.

Detective Barnes: (Suspiciously) Are you sure about that? You stood to gain a lot from her death, didn't you? You would inherit her share of the company.

John Taylor: (Defensively) Yes, but I would never do anything to harm her. I loved her like a sister.

Scene 3: The detective decides to investigate the lab assistants further and discovers that James Parker had access to the poison used to kill Sarah.

Detective Barnes: (Questioning James Parker) Did you have access to the poison used to kill Sarah?

James Parker: (Nervously) Yes, I did. But I swear, I didn't use it on her.

Detective Barnes: (Questioning James Parker) Then why did you have access to it?

James Parker: (Explaining) It was for a research project. I was testing the effects of the poison on cells in a petri dish.

Scene 4: The detective then interviews Dr. Rachel Smith again and finds out that she had been having an affair with John Taylor.

Detective Barnes: (Questioning Dr. Rachel Smith) Did you have any reason to want Sarah dead?

Dr. Rachel Smith: No, of course not. Sarah was my boss and friend. Why would I want to harm her?

Detective Barnes: (Questioning Dr. Rachel Smith) What about your relationship with John Taylor?

Dr. Rachel Smith: (Defensively) What does that have to do with anything?

Detective Barnes: (Accusingly) It has everything to do with it. You had a motive to want Sarah out of the picture so that you could be with John and inherit her share of the company.

Scene 5: The detective pieces together the evidence and confronts the killer.

Detective Barnes: (Addressing the group) I know who killed Sarah. It was Dr. Rachel Smith.

Dr. Rachel Smith: (Surprised) What? That's ridiculous. I would never harm Sarah.

Detective Barnes: (Accusingly) But you had a motive. You wanted her out of the way so that you could be with John and inherit her share of the company.

Dr. Rachel Smith: (Defensively) That's not true. John and I were just friends.

Detective Barnes: (Pointing to the evidence) The evidence says otherwise. You had access to the poison used to kill Sarah, and you were with John when he was discussing the launch of the new drug.

Dr. Rachel Smith: (Breaking down) Okay, fine. I did it. I was in love with John, and I wanted to be with him. Sarah was in the way, and I didn't see any other way out.

Detective Barnes: (Arresting Dr. Rachel Smith) You're under arrest for the murder of Sarah Johnson.

Conclusion: The case is solved, and the killer is brought to justice. Detective Barnes has once again proven his skills as a detective, and justice is served for the victim and her family.

CHAPTER NINE

The Mysterious Death of Mr. Smith

Characters:

Detective Jack Johnson: A seasoned detective who has solved many complicated cases in his career.

Mrs. Elizabeth Smith: The widow of the deceased Mr. Smith.

Mr. Edward Brown: A business partner of Mr. Smith.

Miss Sarah Jones: The deceased's personal assistant.

Mr. Daniel Green: The deceased's lawyer.

Act 1, Scene 1:

(Setting: The living room of Mr. Smith's house. The room is dimly lit. Mrs. Smith is sitting on the couch, crying. Detective Jack Johnson enters the room.)

Detective Jack: Good evening, Mrs. Smith. I am Detective Jack Johnson. I am sorry for your loss. Can you please tell me what happened?

Mrs. Smith: Thank you, Detective. My husband, Mr. Smith, was found dead in his study this morning. I don't know what happened.

Detective Jack: Can you show me the study?

Mrs. Smith: Yes, of course.

(Scene 2: The study)

Detective Jack: (Examining the room) Can you tell me who else had access to this room?

Mrs. Smith: Mr. Edward Brown, my husband's business partner, had access to this room.

Detective Jack: Did you notice anything unusual yesterday?

Mrs. Smith: No, everything was normal.

Detective Jack: I will need to question Mr. Brown. Can you arrange a meeting?

Mrs. Smith: Yes, I will do that.

Act 2, Scene 1:

(Setting: The office of Mr. Edward Brown. Detective Jack enters the room.)

Detective Jack: Good afternoon, Mr. Brown. I am Detective Jack Johnson. I am investigating the death of Mr. Smith.

Mr. Brown: I am shocked to hear about Mr. Smith's death. How can I help you?

Detective Jack: Can you tell me about your relationship with Mr. Smith?

Mr. Brown: We were business partners for the last ten years. We were planning to expand our business.

Detective Jack: Did you have any personal issues with Mr. Smith?

Mr. Brown: No, not at all.

Detective Jack: Did you see or talk to Mr. Smith yesterday?

Mr. Brown: No, I didn't. I was in a meeting with some clients the whole day.

Detective Jack: Can you give me the names of the clients you met with?

Mr. Brown: Yes, of course. (hands over a file to Detective Jack)

Act 3, Scene 1:

(Setting: The deceased's lawyer's office. Detective Jack enters the room.)

Detective Jack: Good morning, Mr. Green. I am Detective Jack Johnson. I am investigating the death of Mr. Smith.

Mr. Green: Yes, I heard about it. Please, take a seat.

Detective Jack: Can you tell me about your relationship with Mr. Smith?

Mr. Green: I was his lawyer for the last fifteen years. He was a very good client.

Detective Jack: Did he mention any personal issues to you?

Mr. Green: No, not at all.

Detective Jack: Did you see or talk to Mr. Smith yesterday?

Mr. Green: Yes, I met him yesterday afternoon to discuss some legal matters.

Detective Jack: Can you give me more details about the meeting?

Mr. Green: Yes, of course. (gives Detective Jack some papers)

Act 4, Scene 1:

(Setting: The deceased's house. Detective Jack is sitting in the living room with Mrs. Smith and Miss Jones.)

Detective Jack: Miss Jones, can you tell me about your relationship with Mr. Smith?

Miss Jones: I was Mr. Smith's personal assistant for the last two years. I helped him with his day-to-day activities and managed his schedule.

Detective Jack: Did Mr. Smith have any enemies or personal issues that he confided in you?

Miss Jones: No, not that I am aware of. He was a very private person.

Detective Jack: Did you notice anything unusual yesterday?

Miss Jones: No, everything was normal. I left the office around 6 PM, and Mr. Smith was still working in his study.

Detective Jack: Thank you, Miss Jones. Mrs. Smith, do you have any information that might be helpful for the investigation?

Mrs. Smith: No, Detective. I am sorry. I still can't believe my husband is gone.

Detective Jack: I understand, Mrs. Smith. I will do everything in my power to find the person responsible for your husband's death. Thank you all for your time. I will keep you updated on the investigation.

(Exit all characters)

Act 5, Scene 1:

(Setting: The detective's office. Detective Jack is going through the files and papers gathered during the investigation.)

Detective Jack: (Muttering to himself) None of the suspects have a clear motive for the murder. It's like Mr. Smith was killed for no reason.

(Phone rings)

Detective Jack: (Answers the phone) Detective Jack Johnson speaking.

Caller: Hello, Detective. This is Mr. Brown. I need to talk to you about something important.

Detective Jack: Yes, Mr. Brown. What is it?

Mr. Brown: I think I know who killed Mr. Smith.

Detective Jack: (Surprised) What? Who is it?

Mr. Brown: It's Miss Jones. I saw her leaving the house around 7 PM yesterday, carrying a bag. It looked like she was in a hurry.

Detective Jack: Thank you, Mr. Brown. You have been very helpful.

(Ends the call)

Act 6, Scene 1:

(Setting: The police station. Miss Jones is sitting in the interrogation room. Detective Jack enters the room.)

Detective Jack: Miss Jones, we have evidence that suggests that you were involved in Mr. Smith's murder.

Miss Jones: (Panicking) What? No, I didn't do anything. I loved Mr. Smith. He was like a father figure to me.

Detective Jack: Mr. Brown saw you leaving the house around 7 PM yesterday, carrying a bag.

Miss Jones: (Nervously) Yes, I left the house around that time, but it was because Mr. Smith asked me to deliver some papers to his lawyer. I was in a hurry, so I didn't tell anyone.

Detective Jack: (Skeptical) Do you have any proof of this?

Miss Jones: (Handing over the papers) Here are the papers Mr. Smith asked me to deliver.

Detective Jack: (Examining the papers) These papers do match the ones Mr. Green gave me. I apologize for the inconvenience, Miss Jones. You are free to go.

(Exit Miss Jones)

Act 7, Scene 1:

(Setting: The detective's office. Detective Jack is sitting at his desk, looking at the evidence.)

Detective Jack: (Muttering to himself) If Miss Jones didn't kill Mr. Smith, then who did?

(Phone rings)

Detective Jack: (Answers the phone) Detective Jack Johnson speaking.

Caller: Hello, Detective. This is Mrs. Smith. I think I know who killed my husband.

Detective Jack: (Surprised) Really? Who is it?

Mrs. Smith: It's Mr.

(Phone disconnects)

Detective Jack: (Puzzled) Mr. who? (Trying to call back but there is no answer)

Act 7, Scene 2:

(Setting: The police station. Detective Jack is speaking to his colleague, Detective Brown.)

Detective Jack: Mrs. Smith just called me and said she knows who killed her husband but the call got disconnected before she could tell me the name.

Detective Brown: That's strange. Did you try calling her back?

Detective Jack: Yes, but she didn't answer. I have a feeling that this might be our breakthrough. Let's go to her house and see if we can find anything useful.

Act 8, Scene 1:

(Setting: Mrs. Smith's living room. Detectives Jack and Brown are searching for clues.)

Detective Jack: (Looking at a photo on the wall) Who is this?

Mrs. Smith: (Entering the room) That's my husband with his business partner, Mr. John.

Detective Jack: (Interested) Mr. John? Do you have his contact information?

Mrs. Smith: Yes, I do. He was one of my husband's closest friends.

Detective Brown: (Finding something under the sofa) Look at this.

Detective Jack: (Examining the item) This is a knife with bloodstains. Mrs. Smith, can you tell us where this came from?

Mrs. Smith: (Shocked) I don't know. I have never seen that before.

Detective Jack: (Dialing a number on his phone) We need to bring Mr. John in for questioning.

Act 9, Scene 1:

(Setting: The interrogation room. Mr. John is sitting at the table with Detectives Jack and Brown.)

Detective Jack: Mr. John, we found a knife with bloodstains in Mrs. Smith's house. Do you know anything about it?

Mr. John: (Nervously) No, I don't. Why are you asking me?

Detective Jack: We have reason to believe that you were involved in the murder of Mr. Smith.

Mr. John: (Panicking) What? No, that's not true. I didn't do anything.

Detective Brown: We have evidence that suggests otherwise, Mr. John. We found your fingerprints on the knife.

Mr. John: (Sighing) Okay, fine. I did it. Mr. Smith and I had some disagreements about the business, and I just lost it. I didn't mean to kill him.

Detective Jack: (Disgusted) You just admitted to murder. You're under arrest.

(Exit Detectives and Mr. John)

Act 10, Scene 1:

(Setting: Mrs. Smith's living room. Mrs. Smith is sitting on the sofa, crying. Detective Jack enters the room.)

Detective Jack: Mrs. Smith, I am sorry for your loss. We have arrested the person responsible for your husband's death.

Mrs. Smith: (Thankful) Thank you, Detective. I don't know what I would do without your help.

Detective Jack: (Smiling) It's my job. I'm just glad we were able to bring closure to this case. If you need anything else you can call me.

CHAPTER TEN

The Mysterious Death at Westwind Manor

Characters:

Detective James Smith: The lead detective in charge of the investigation

Mr. Edward Westwind: The wealthy owner of Westwind Manor

Mrs. Emily Westwind: The deceased's wife and a prime suspect

Dr. David Brown: The family physician and a potential suspect

Ms. Victoria Black: The deceased's personal assistant and a potential suspect

Mr. Mark Williams: The deceased's business partner and a potential suspect

Mrs. Samantha Green: The deceased's former lover and a potential suspect

Act 1: The scene opens with Detective James Smith arriving at Westwind Manor, a grand estate nestled in the English countryside. He is greeted by Mr. Edward Westwind, the owner of the estate, who informs him that his wife, Mrs. Emily Westwind, has been found dead in the library. The detective immediately orders the area to be secured and sets about interviewing the suspects.

Detective James Smith: Mr. Westwind, I'm sorry for your loss. Can you tell me when you last saw your wife?

Mr. Edward Westwind: It was around 9 PM last night. We had dinner together, and then she retired to the library to read.

Detective James Smith: And what did you do after that?

Mr. Edward Westwind: I retired to my room. I was feeling a bit under the weather.

Detective James Smith: I see. Can you give me a list of people who had access to the library last night?

Mr. Edward Westwind: My wife's personal assistant, Ms. Victoria Black, and her former lover, Mrs. Samantha Green, were both here. Also, Dr. David Brown, the family physician, came by to see my wife.

Detective James Smith: I'd like to speak to each of them. Please have them brought here.

Act 2: As the detective begins his investigation, the suspects are interrogated one by one.

Detective James Smith: Ms. Black, can you tell me what you were doing in the library last night?

Ms. Victoria Black: I was checking Mrs. Westwind's schedule for the week.

Detective James Smith: And did you see anyone else in the library?

Ms. Victoria Black: No, I didn't.

Detective James Smith: Dr. Brown, did you have any interaction with Mrs. Westwind last night?

Dr. David Brown: Yes, I did. I came to check on her. She was complaining of a headache.

Detective James Smith: And did you see anyone else in the library?

Dr. David Brown: No, I didn't.

Detective James Smith: Mrs. Green, can you tell me why you were here last night?

Mrs. Samantha Green: I came to return a book to Mrs. Westwind. We were still friends, you know.

Detective James Smith: And did you see anyone else in the library?

Mrs. Samantha Green: No, I didn't.

Detective James Smith: Mr. Williams, what can you tell me about your business dealings with Mr. Westwind?

Mr. Mark Williams: We've been partners for years. We run a successful publishing company.

Detective James Smith: Did you see Mrs. Westwind last night?

Mr. Mark Williams: No, I didn't. I left the estate early.

Act 3: As the investigation progresses, the detective begins to piece together the clues.

Detective James Smith: Mr. Westwind, I believe I have solved the case.

Mr. Edward Westwind: You have? Who is the killer?

Detective James Smith: It was Mrs. Emily Westwind's personal assistant, Ms. Victoria Black.

Ms. Victoria Black: What?! That's ridiculous! I didn't kill Mrs. Westwind!

Detective James Smith: The evidence suggests otherwise. Firstly, you had access to the library last night. Secondly, we found traces of poison in Mrs. Westwind's tea cup, and the poison was found in your possession.

Ms. Victoria Black: That's preposterous! I never poisoned anyone! I always carry those herbs with me for my personal use.

Detective James Smith: And yet, you were the only one who had the opportunity and the means to commit this crime. Mrs. Westwind was about to fire you for embezzlement, and you couldn't afford to lose your job.

Ms. Victoria Black: I didn't embezzle anything! It's a lie!

Mr. Edward Westwind: Detective, are you sure about this? Ms. Black has been with us for years. I can't believe she would do something like this.

Detective James Smith: I'm sure, Mr. Westwind. The evidence is clear. Ms. Black, you are under arrest for the murder of Mrs. Emily Westwind.

Ms. Victoria Black: No! This can't be happening! You're making a mistake!

As Ms. Victoria Black is led away in handcuffs, the others watch in shock. Detective James Smith turns to Mr. Westwind.

Detective James Smith: I'm sorry for your loss, Mr. Westwind. But we will bring justice for your wife.

The curtain falls as the sound of the jail cell door slamming shut echoes through the theater.

Detective James Smith: Wait a minute. Something doesn't add up here. Ms. Victoria Black may not be the murderer after all.

Ms. Victoria Black: Thank you, detective! I told you I didn't do it!

Detective James Smith: I apologize for jumping to conclusions, Ms. Black. It's just that the evidence seemed so convincing.

Mr. Edward Westwind: So if it wasn't Ms. Black, who could have killed my wife?

Detective James Smith: I'm not sure yet, but I have a feeling that Dr. David Brown might have something to do with it.

Dr. David Brown: What?! I would never harm my patient!

Detective James Smith: We found traces of a rare poison in Mrs. Westwind's system. It's a poison that is commonly used in medical practice, but it's not something that you would normally prescribe for a headache. And yet, you were the last person to see Mrs. Westwind alive.

Dr. David Brown: I swear I didn't do it!

Detective James Smith: I'll need to investigate further, but for now, I'm placing you under arrest for the murder of Mrs. Emily Westwind.

As Dr. Brown is led away in handcuffs, the others look on in shock.

Mr. Mark Williams: I can't believe it. Dr. Brown was always so kind to Mrs. Westwind.

Mrs. Samantha Green: This is all so tragic. Poor Mrs. Westwind.

Mr. Edward Westwind: Thank you, detective, for bringing the killer to justice. But I still can't believe that anyone would want to harm my wife.

Detective James Smith: Unfortunately, Mr. Westwind, sometimes even the people closest to us can be capable of terrible things. But we will do everything in our power to find out why Dr. Brown did what he did and bring him to justice.

As the curtain falls, the audience is left wondering what could have driven Dr. Brown to commit such a heinous crime.

Detective James Smith returns to the stage, carrying a file folder.

Detective James Smith: Ladies and gentlemen, we have uncovered the motive for the murder of Mrs. Emily Westwind.

Mr. Edward Westwind: Please, detective, tell us what you have found.

Detective James Smith: It appears that Dr. David Brown was in dire financial straits. He had accumulated a large amount of debt due to gambling and was facing possible bankruptcy. He knew that Mrs. Westwind was a wealthy woman, and he saw an opportunity to solve his financial problems by taking her life.

Ms. Victoria Black: That's just terrible. How could someone do such a thing?

Detective James Smith: It's hard to say, Ms. Black. But unfortunately, greed and desperation can drive people to commit horrible acts.

Mr. Mark Williams: So what will happen to Dr. Brown now?

Detective James Smith: He will be prosecuted to the fullest extent of the law. And I hope that this serves as a warning to anyone who might consider taking a life for financial gain.

The audience applauds as Detective James Smith takes his final bow. As the curtains close, the actors take their final positions on stage, and the lights fade to black, leaving the audience to reflect on the tragic events that have just unfolded.